CODE BREAKERS AND SPIES

Code Breakers and Spies of
the War on Terror

ELIZABETH SCHMERMUND

Cavendish Square
New York

Published in 2019 by Cavendish Square Publishing, LLC
243 5th Avenue, Suite 136, New York, NY 10016

Copyright © 2019 by Cavendish Square Publishing, LLC

First Edition

No part of this publication may be reproduced, stored in a retrieval system, or transmitted in any form or by any means—electronic, mechanical, photocopying, recording, or otherwise—without the prior permission of the copyright owner. Request for permission should be addressed to Permissions, Cavendish Square Publishing, 243 5th Avenue, Suite 136, New York, NY 10016. Tel (877) 980-4450; fax (877) 980-4454.

Website: cavendishsq.com

This publication represents the opinions and views of the author based on his or her personal experience, knowledge, and research. The information in this book serves as a general guide only. The author and publisher have used their best efforts in preparing this book and disclaim liability rising directly or indirectly from the use and application of this book.

All websites were available and accurate when this book was sent to press.

Library of Congress Cataloging-in-Publication Data

Names: Schmermund, Elizabeth.
Title: Code breakers and spies of the war on terror / Elizabeth Schmermund.
Description: New York : Cavendish Square, 2019. | Series: Code breakers and spies | Includes glossary and index.
Identifiers: ISBN 9781502638632 (pbk.) | ISBN 9781502638625 (library bound) | ISBN 9781502638649 (ebook)
Subjects: LCSH: Espionage--Juvenile literature. | War on Terrorism, 2001-2009--Technology--Juvenile literature. | Technological innovations--History--21st century--Juvenile literature. | Terrorism--United States--Prevention--Juvenile literature.
Classification: LCC HV6431.S36 2019 | DDC 363.325'160973--dc23

Editorial Director: David McNamara
Editor: Stacy Orlando
Copy Editor: Alex Tessman
Associate Art Director: Amy Greenan
Designer: Joe Parenteau
Production Coordinator: Karol Szymczuk
Photo Research: J8 Media

The photographs in this book are used by permission and through the courtesy of: Cover Erik Simonsen/Photographer's Choice/Getty Images; p. 4 Bettmann/Getty Images; p. 7 Bletchley Park Trust/SSPL/Getty Images; p. 10 Watford/Mirrorpix/Getty Images; p. 13 DOD/Getty Images; p. 16 Spencer Platt/Getty Images; p. 19 Universal History Archive/Getty Images; p. 22 Mark Wilson/Getty Images; p. 27 Kae CH/Shutterstock.com; p. 30 Trinacria Photo/Shutterstock.co; p. 32 /Wikimedia Commons/File:Mostwanted Iraqi playing cards 06.jpg/CC0 1.0 Public Domain; p. 34 US Air Force/Corbis/Getty Images; p. 37 John McDonnell/The Washington Post/Getty Images; p. 39 Bryan Bedder/Getty Images/OUT Magazine; p. 41 Barton Gellman/Getty Images; p. 46 Saeed Shah/MCT via Getty Images; p. 53 Courtesy Costs of War Project, Watson Institute for International & Public Affairs, Brown University; p.54 Harry Hamburg/NY Daily News Archive/Getty Images; p. 61 NYU; p. 65 Titikul_B/Shutterstock.com; p. 68 Scott Olson/Getty Images; p. 71 Daniel Leal-Olivas/AFP/Getty Images.

Printed in the United States of America

Contents

1 Burgeoning Technology............5

2 The War on Terror................17

3 Victory and Defeat...............31

4 Impact and Legacy...............55

Chronology........................72

Glossary..........................73

Further Information...............75

Selected Bibliography.............76

Index.............................78

About the Author..................80

CHAPTER 1

BURGEONING TECHNOLOGY

Since the middle of the twentieth century, modern technology has undergone a revolution. Inventions that were once figments in the imagination of science fiction writers have become integral parts of our daily lives. Computers, mobile devices, and the internet connect people around the globe. Satellites encircling the earth gather and transmit an enormous amount of information, and can even take high-resolution pictures of anyone, anywhere, and pinpoint their exact location.

OPPOSITE: Satellites, which orbit around the earth, can collect and transmit data for the purposes of surveillance and spying.

Of course, many people use this technology to interact with friends, or to post activities on social media. But these new forms of technology are also incredibly important in the military and on the political world stage. In fact, many of the popular technological advances used today were probably invented—at least, in part—to be used to spy on or fight against other countries and political enemies. One of the biggest motivations for developing new technologies has long been security and warfare.

Computing and War Making

The first mechanical computer was developed by Charles Babbage in the early nineteenth century. After losing funding from the British government, however, Babbage's machine didn't gain the popularity or momentum he had wanted. Several other inventors also began to work on developing computers, to some success. However, in 1938, it was the United States Navy that began to develop computers more similar to the ones we use today. Computer scientists and engineers in the Navy developed an electromechanical analog computer that was small enough to be used on a submarine. The purpose of this new machine was to aid torpedo firing and make it more accurate against enemies.

Colossus, shown here in 1943, was the world's first electronic programmable computer.

Colossus

Advancements in computing took even greater strides during World War II, when it became more necessary to develop machines that could aid in the war. On the Axis side, German engineer Arthur Scherbius built another form of electromechanical computer, called a cipher machine, which could transfer military messages in code. This became known as an Enigma machine and was a major part of the military strategy for Germany and its allies. The Allied powers—led in this effort by Great Britain—sprung to develop their own machinery to break the Enigma code in order to gain intelligence over their enemies and win the war.

Efforts took place largely in Bletchley Park in Buckinghamshire, England. There, early computer

Burgeoning Technology 7

scientists, mathematicians, engineers, and even those skilled at puzzles worked tirelessly to decode the Enigma communications through building their own kind of computer capable of translating the message. This led to the invention of the Colossus, the world's first electronic digital programmable computer. Colossus was named for its size, as it used many vacuum tubes, had many knobs and inputs, and was large enough to fill a wall. Eventually, Colossus became famous for doing what it had been designed to do—break the Enigma code. In 1941, German operators mistakenly sent out two versions of the same message. The mistake gave the Colossus operators enough information for the computer to decrypt the message. From then on, Great Britain and its allies collected important high-level military intelligence for the duration of the war, without the German military—or anyone else—ever knowing. Colossus was kept secret until the mid-1970s.

The US DoD . . . and Text Messaging?

The US Department of Defense (DoD) was responsible for another important technology that we use almost every day: the internet. Developed in the late 1960s, the internet was first used, like the computer itself, for espionage.

The first prototype of what would become the internet was known as the Advanced Research Projects Agency Network, or ARPANET. It allowed multiple computers to communicate on a single network. Agents in the US DoD needed to share classified material without worrying that it would fall prey to anyone else. ARPANET was later refined by the use of the Transmission Control Protocol and Internet Protocol (TCP/IP), which set protocols for how messages and information could be exchanged by computers not only in one system, but across multiple systems. This was released on January 1, 1983. Soon, computer programmers had worked to assemble many networks together using these protocols—this would become the World Wide Web, which was released to the public in 1990.

Mobile Messages

The first text messaging system was conceived during the Cold War in the 1960s, way before most people had access even to a handheld phone. The Central Intelligence Agency (CIA) developed a wireless communication system, called Short-Range Agent Communications, or SRAC, to allow agents to send

Wireless communication devices hidden in satchels were originally bulky and could cause spies to be discovered.

secret messages to one another, as long as they were in close proximity. Early uses involved shoebox-sized base stations that would probably have gotten spies more attention than they would have wanted! In time, these technologies evolved and devices got smaller, but they were not without problems. For instance, both the sender and the receiver had to remain still while the message was transmitted, and though small, the blinking red light on the device put a spy's cover in danger.

Spying Techniques in the Gulf

Espionage and spy methodologies evolved even further as a result of the massive influx of electronic innovations during the 1990s. The decade began with a military action that sent shock waves around the globe—Iraqi president Saddam Hussein sent forces into the small neighboring country of Kuwait in August 1990. His purpose was to claim the country—and its oil reserves—for Iraq. Many nations, including the United States, decided that they could not sit by while a country was overthrown by a powerful dictator without taking action. So, in January of 1991, the United States led a coalition into Kuwait and Iraq in what was labeled Operation Desert Storm, and later known as the Gulf War.

The war would prove to be incredibly brief, lasting just over four days, and has been referred to as the 100 hours' war. Coalition troops effectively removed Iraqi forces from Kuwait and liberated the small country from its larger and more powerful neighbor. For the Iraqis, it was a decisive loss. Approximately 20,000 Iraqi soldiers were killed during those several days, while 148 United States soldiers lost their lives.

The Albert Sombolay Case

In 1991, the case of an exposed spy drew attention across the globe. Albert Sombolay was an American soldier who participated in the Gulf War. According to the US military's official statement, "During an investigation prior to his arrest, Sombolay had told an undercover agent he had initiated contact with the Jordanian and Iraqi embassies in Belgium and Germany in December 1990." The Army also stated that Sombolay had told the Iraqis and Jordanians that he would photograph his unit's activities in Saudi Arabia in the lead-up to the invasion of Kuwait. Sombolay pled guilty to charges of espionage and contacting the enemy. He was eventually convicted and sentenced to thirty years in prison. What did he get in return from his spying activities? Sources say that he was paid about $1,300 by Iraqi officials, a small sum especially when viewed in terms of his long prison sentence.

Digital Assistance

Many people point to new technology as the evident reason why the Western forces had won this conflict so quickly. For one, the United States used precision guided munitions (PGMs) for the first time. These "smart bombs" utilized laser guidance systems and satellite localization to steer into targets. Tomahawk cruise missiles and F-117 Stealth fighter-bombers were forms of new aircraft that were invisible to Iraqi radar, allowing them to sneak into Iraqi air space without raising a red flag.

In addition to new weaponry and targeting systems, advances in satellite localization and early applications of a Global Positioning System (GPS) allowed the

US Marines use satellite communication during Operation Desert Storm in order to transmit video to the Pentagon.

US military to see exactly where their enemies were in comparison to their own troops. According to Professor Robert M. Citino, "reading data from orbiting satellites, they relayed precise coordinate locations to the user on the ground, allowing him to plot artillery fire, to compute bearings to his objective, to measure an aircraft's angle of descent, and much more. Satellite technology also provided intelligence to headquarters at all levels, gathering, processing, and transmitting it almost instantaneously through the new Joint Surveillance Target Attack Radar System (JSTARS). This allowed the US Army in Operation Desert Storm to gather correct information upon which to build their intelligence, which had been lacking in previous wars."

Other forms of technology filled in what few gaps remained in intelligence. For example, Apache helicopters used thermal-sight sensors that picked up differences in heat high up above the ground. The sensors allowed US troops to "see" in the pitch black and continue fighting through the night. If a certain temperature of heat was detected, it would likely mean the presence of humans in that area. Due, in part, to this technology, coalition forces destroyed at least 3,847 out of 4,280 Iraqi tanks during combat over these few days.

DID YOU KNOW?

In the 1970s, the CIA's Office of Research and Development created a micro Unmanned Aerial Vehicle (UAV), disguised as a dragonfly, in order to collect intelligence secretly.

Satellite technology played a large and important role in the first Gulf War, and yet it was still in its infancy and had many limitations. Spy satellites could gather much-needed intelligence, but often there was a long lag time between the satellite taking pictures and sending them to field officers and forces. Even just several hours could be too long. For example, a spy satellite could pick out where troops or a particular enemy combatant was located, but by the time the picture was taken and transmitted to the nearest US troops, the "target" could have moved on and the intelligence would become useless. The margin of error was also too great to launch missiles against a target seen on a spy satellite.

CHAPTER 2

THE WAR ON TERROR

The large-scale attacks which mark the start of the war on terror stem from a major failing of US intelligence. On September 11, 2001, terrorists hijacked and then piloted commercial planes, crashing them into the World Trade Center and the Pentagon. A third plane went down in Shanksville, Pennsylvania, after a passenger uprising stopped the terrorists from flying the plane into a more populated area. This unprecedented series of events injured over 6,000 people, took the lives of 2,977 more, and were responsible for at least $10 billion in damages.

OPPOSITE: Many claim the terrorist attacks on September 11, 2001 were successfully carried out due to a failure in US intelligence gathering.

Enemy of the West

Within hours after the attacks, a man named Osama bin Laden, the Saudi head of a terrorist organization known as al-Qaeda, was believed to be the mastermind behind the attacks. Further investigations revealed the identities of the nineteen hijackers who had put the plan into action. The fact that bin Laden's group had wanted to launch attacks on America had long been evident, and already had some success. In 1993, al-Qaeda trained operatives exploded a truck bomb in the underground parking lot of the World Trade Center, killing six people and injuring over one thousand.

The animosity of al-Qaeda toward America had been known since bin Laden issued statements condemning US foreign policy starting around 1996. Al-Qaeda members had even publically declared that they wanted to bring down the towers, once and for all. In addition, information about training the attackers received and communications between their ties and the larger terrorist organization had been obtained by US intelligence agencies before the attacks. The US intelligence community was certainly aware of the threat al-Qaeda posed to the United States and issued a report in February 2001. In it, officials wrote that bin Laden's terrorist organization was "the most immediate and serious threat" to the United States, and that they were capable of "planning multiple attacks with little or no warning." Unfortunately, most of these warnings—some of which came from within the US intelligence community itself—went unheeded.

Osama bin Laden was the founder of al-Qaeda.

A New Dawn of Intelligence

Following the largest terrorist offensive within American borders, the 9/11 Commission, an unbiased, third-party review committee, was formed in 2002. Following a series of investigations, the commission issued their findings on the attacks and what could have been done to prevent the incidents. The 2004 9/11 Commission Report noted that the intelligence community had failed to act upon information they received, due in part because they received "an overwhelming number of priorities, flat budgets, an outmoded structure, and bureaucratic rivalries." In particular, there was little communication between field agents, bureaucrats, and elected officials, especially between government agencies, such as the CIA, the National Security Agency (NSA), and the Federal Bureau of Investigations (FBI).

Patriot Act

In order to rectify this problem, Congress approved the Intelligence Reform and Terrorism Prevention Act in 2004, which created the Director of National Intelligence (DNI) position, and the National Counterterrorism Center (NCTC). The NCTC pools intelligence from multiple national and international agencies, and coordinates efforts. Prior to this, the USA Patriot Act (Uniting and Strengthening America by Providing Appropriate Tools Required to Intercept and Obstruct Terrorism Act) was signed into law on October 24, 2001. This Act was written in order to allow intelligence officers within the United States and beyond to collect private information on suspected terrorists more easily.

Following the passage of the Patriot Act, certain circumstances would allow investigators to search a home or office without the owner's consent, and enable the FBI to obtain telephone, email, and financial records without a court order, which had previously been necessary. Law enforcement officers also had more access to business records and formerly private

> **DID YOU KNOW?**
>
> Certain provisions of the Patriot Act were subject to deadlines, or sunsets, and many were reauthorized, expanded, or made permanent through 2019 with the passage of the USA Freedom Act in 2015.

information such as what books a person checked out of the library or what they searched for on their computers. Advanced computer and internet spy algorithms, developed by US intelligence in order to fight against terrorism, allowed for even more new forms of intelligence gathering.

The War on Terror Begins

On September 16, 2001, just five days after the terrorist attacks, US President George W. Bush announced the beginning of a "war on terror" against "a radical network of terrorists and every government that supports them." Four days later, Bush gave an ultimatum to the Taliban government in Afghanistan, who had been harboring Osama bin Laden and other al-Qaeda leaders. If Afghanistan did not turn over these terrorists, Bush stated, the United States

Former US President George W. Bush addresses the nation following the attacks on September 11, 2001.

would attack. The Taliban did not comply with Bush's demands and, in October 2001, US forces and their allies began an invasion of Afghanistan, which became known as Operation Enduring Freedom, or more simply, the War in Afghanistan.

From Afghanistan to Iraq

Shortly after the War in Afghanistan began, the United States turned its sights to Iraq, where Saddam Hussein still ruled the country. The Bush administration attempted to prove that Hussein's government was involved in the September 11 terrorist attacks, and that they possessed nuclear arms, or weapons of mass destruction (WMDs). Although these claims were later proven to be false, the invasion of Iraq began in March 2003. The aim of the military strategy labeled Operation Iraqi Freedom was to secure the area from terrorists and to topple the Hussein regime. Hussein fled along with top Iraqi officials and was captured in December of that year.

While the official War in Afghanistan and the War in Iraq drew to a close in 2011 and 2014, respectively, the war on terror has continued in these countries and other nations in the region. The war on terror has led to US military involvement in Yemen and northwest Pakistan, to name a few. In addition, the rise of the Islamic State (IS), a group that emerged from al-Qaeda following the Iraq War, led to a new phase of war across many countries in the Middle East, including Iraq, Syria, and Libya. From the end of 2014 on, a new mission in Afghanistan began, called Operation Freedom's Sentinel, in which US military efforts would be focused both on supporting the Afghan military and ensuring that the country would not serve again as a base of operations for terrorist activities.

Global Spread of Intelligence

The military campaigns of the war on terror have not just been fought on the battlefield. In fact, more than ever before, the bulk of military action has hinged on spy and espionage activities conducted to prevent or to prepare for physical encounters between enemy combatants. Global intelligence communities recruited new members who could speak languages such as Arabic and Urdu, or who could fit into a certain culture or landscape. They also hired hordes of computer scientists, technology officials, and even hackers in order to use computer-based technologies to spy on potential terrorism-related communications.

By 2010, according to a report by the *Washington Post*, there were more than 1,200 government organizations and 1,900 private companies "working on counterterrorism, homeland security, and intelligence in some 10,000 locations across the United States." The report called the amount of government employees working in surveillance and intelligence gathering "unwieldy" and noted that "854,000 people—or nearly one and one-half times the number of people who live in Washington—have top-secret security clearance." These figures represent the efforts of the United States alone, and America has not been alone in the war on terror.

Spy Technologies

New recruits were brought in by intelligence agencies in order to "find new ways to bring science to bear in the war on terrorism." Technological advancements over the last two decades have little resemblance to the old, clunky machines used in World War II and the Cold War. Rather, the spy technology used during the global war on terror is smaller, more discreet, and more powerful. UAVs can fly over large swaths of territory without being tracked by traditional radar, and use cameras with incredibly high resolutions able to capture images of individual people from thousands of feet above the ground. Operators of the drones can be located thousands of miles away from danger, piloting the vehicles remotely.

According to Greg Davis, the projects applications manager who worked on several UAV projects, most UAVs come with both infrared and television cameras that can provide real-time video, which can be streamed back to Langley Air Force Base, in Virginia. Real-life operators can tell a UAV to track an individual object—including a person—with the click of a mouse. In addition, multiple UAVs can work together in order to pick up and track a car or person who is moving rapidly from one area

Drones, Drones Everywhere

Ranging from the size of your thumb to the size of an iPad or more, remote-controlled toy drones can take off and land, fly at speeds greater than 30 miles per hour (50 kilometers per hour), take weather data, and capture and send pictures and video. These small fliers can range in price from thirty to thousands of dollars. Machines come in a variety of shapes as well; even styled like the Millennium Falcon from *Star Wars*!

Unmanned aerial vehicles (UAVs) have been utilized to take high-resolution photos of enemy combatants without being detected, and unmanned combat aerial vehicles (UCAVs) are equipped with weapons. Today's military drones can have wingspans of 130 feet (40 meters) and weigh up to 15,000 pounds (6,800 kilograms). The United States alone has spent billions of dollars purchasing and developing spy planes. Newly developed drones, like the A160 Hummingbird, will be equipped with a system called the Autonomous Real-time Ground Ubiquitous Surveillance-Imaging System (Argus-IS), which can track people and vehicles from altitudes above 20,000 feet (6,096 m) across almost 65 square miles (168 square kilometers). Unlike toy drones, these drones fly at around 230 mph (370 kmh)!

Although they share a name, toy drones have little in common with military drones, also known as UAVs.

Although children and people of all ages may enjoy playing with toy drones, they are not without hazard; in fact, they can become quite dangerous if not used correctly. Toy drones have been known to interfere with radio control towers; crash into airplanes, helicopters, and cars; and cause accidental injuries and even deaths. There have also been accounts of drones used to smuggle drugs. Because of incidents like these, toy drones are becoming more tightly regulated by governments. Before sending that new toy into the sky, be sure to check local regulations around flying recreational drones.

to another. The American military uses UAVs with high-tech surveillance to monitor potential terrorists actions and movements.

Vulnerable Systems

In 2013, a former information technology (IT) specialist named Edward Snowden, who worked for the CIA, copied and leaked top-secret information and released it to the public. This information confirmed the surveillance that US intelligence agencies undertook in the name of preventing terrorism. These disclosures showed not only the extent of the US government's spying on ordinary citizens, but a network of countries with which the United States shared data and vice versa. Many companies were also involved in this data collection, including phone companies, internet companies like Google and Facebook, and computer manufacturers like Apple and Microsoft.

Later releases by WikiLeaks (an international non-profit launched in 2006 by Julian Assange) showed that the CIA used many advanced hacking tools, including inserting undetectable bugs into Apple computers that could not be erased, and that would send all information from the computer to the

> **DID YOU KNOW?**
>
> The largest release of classified US military documents to date occurred in 2010 when WikiLeaks made close to 400,000 reports, known as The Iraq War Logs, available to the public.

CIA. According to WikiLeaks, "While CIA assets are sometimes used to physically infect systems in the custody of a target, it is likely that many CIA physical access attacks have infected the targeted organization's supply chain including by interdicting mail orders and other shipments."

CASPIAN SEA
USTYURT PLATEAU
Kyzyl (Desert)
Kum
Darya
Bishkek
KYRGYZSTAN
Osh
Kokand
Khiva
Tashkent
Kara (Desert)
Kum
UZBEKISTAN
Samarqand
TAJIKISTAN
Dushanbe
Shaki
AZERBAIJAN
Baku
Turkmenbashi
TURKMENISTAN
Chärjew
Bukhoro
Termez
Ashgabat
Mary
Amu
Darya
HINDU KUSH
Tabriz
Rasht
Mashhad
Gushgy
Mazar-e-Sharif
Kabul
Lake Urmia
ELBURZ MTS.
Babol
Mt. Damavand 18,612'
Herat
Qazvin
Tehran
Dasht-e Kavir
Kashmar
AFGHANISTAN
Qom
(Desert)
Hamadan
IRAN
Farah
Baghdad
Birjand
Helmand
BABYLON
Isfahan
Dasht-e Lut (Desert)
Shushtar
Yazd
Ahwaz
PERSEPOLIS
Kerman
Zahedan
PAK
Abadan
Basra
Shiraz
KUWAIT
Bandar-e Bushehr
Bandar-e Abbas
Iranshahr
Kuwait
Persian
Jask
Gwadar
BAHRAIN
Gulf
Strait of Hormuz
Gulf of Oman
Dhahran
Doha
ARABIA
Abu Dhabi
Matrah
Riyadh
QATAR
UNITED ARAB EMIRATES
Muscat
Sur
ARABIAN PENINSULA
Masira I.
Rub Al Khali
[Empty Quarter]
Duym
Makkah]
(UNDEFINED BORDERS)
OMAN
Kuria Muria Is.
Mirbat
Damqawt
Salalah
Sa'dah
Sanaa
YEMEN
Qishn
Al Mukalla
Tamrida

CHAPTER 3
VICTORY AND DEFEAT

While the US military and its allies conducted official wars in both Afghanistan and Iraq, the war on terror became global as intelligence agencies around the world searched for terrorists and strove to prevent attacks. This means that the United States did not restrict reconnaissance efforts and military attacks to Afghanistan and Iraq alone. As part of the new global war on terror, the US military planned surveillance missions and attacks in areas of Pakistan, Yemen, Libya, Syria, and Somalia. Some of these top-secret missions were not even known to the governments in the countries where they were carried out.

OPPOSITE:
US military action and surveillance conducted as part of the war on terror takes place in many countries across the Middle East.

Massive Manhunts

During the 2003 invasion of Iraq, the US military created and distributed sets of playing cards depicting the faces of the most-wanted members of Saddam Hussein's government. The cards not only helped US intelligence and military members identify targets, but also classified the importance of the individuals by the type of card that bore their information. The ace of spades was Saddam Hussein, while other aces in the deck corresponded to his two sons and his presidential secretary. By the end of the war in 2011, most of those featured on the cards had been captured or killed.

Playing cards like these helped US troops to identify the most wanted high-ranking men in Hussein's government.

Cards have been used as a tool for troops on the ground to learn the names and faces of wanted men going back to the Civil War. But identifying important members of the Iraqi military also came from intelligence gathered high up in the sky—from drones. The General Atomics MQ-a Predator, known simply as the Predator, was initially developed during the Gulf War and was upgraded for the wars in Afghanistan and Iraq. Before being retired in 2017, the Predator could fly up to 460 mi (740 km) to reach a target, where it could hover for up to fourteen hours before returning to base. For the war on terror, the Predator was also upgraded to fire Hellfire missiles, which are precision-guided missiles that can target a place on the ground from thousands of feet in the air. The crewmembers that operate these drones, sometimes from bases thousands of miles away, are also trained to analyze what they see and to report anything suspicious to intelligence officers.

The Age of Drones

Predators were tested for the first time early in the war, when a CIA-led secret mission sought a man named Mullah Mohammed Omar. Omar was the commander of the Taliban in Afghanistan and was wanted for protecting Osama bin Laden after the September 11 attacks. Almost immediately after the attacks, the US military decided not to send in ground troops right away, but rather to send in Special Forces and CIA agents. These groups worked with anti-Taliban militias in Afghanistan to search for Taliban leaders. Using drones, CIA agents discovered Omar living in the city of Kandahar.

First Drone Strike

On the night of October 7, Predator video showed Omar leaving his house and entering a building next door. The feed was being viewed in multiple locations by: the CIA and men controlling the

Predator drones were used extensively at the beginning of the wars in Iraq and Afghanistan.

vehicle at Langley, Virginia; US Central Command (CENTCOM) in Tampa, Florida; the Air Force at the Pentagon, Washington, DC; and finally by the Combined Air Operations Center (CAOC) based near the capital of Saudi Arabia. Yet not all locations were actually able to view the feed in real time. To make matters more confusing, the CAOC was supposed to be in charge of all air attacks in Afghanistan, but CENTCOM had control of any orders to the Predator operators to fire.

The CIA and CENTCOM could bomb the house through the remote-powered drone and kill Omar, but such a thing had never done before, and the Air Force already had a fighter aircraft nearby. Nevertheless, the order came over the radio to fire, and the drone pilot launched the missile. Unfortunately, the missile missed its target and hit a car on the street outside of Omar's building instead, allowing the Taliban leader to escape. This was a huge error and many in the US government, military, and intelligence agencies were initially unsure about how to proceed with drone warfare.

However, by the next month, at least forty drone strikes had been carried out in Afghanistan—and the number would grow quickly. Very early on during Operation Enduring Freedom, the US military and its allies toppled the Taliban. Yet even with the new technology at work, many Taliban members (including Osama bin Laden) escaped into the neighboring country of Pakistan, where they remained in hideouts in the rural mountains, and a Taliban resurgence followed.

War and Tragedy

In national elections in September 2005, Hamid Karzai was named the new president of Afghanistan. By October 2006, the intergovernmental military alliance between North American and European countries known as the North Atlantic Treaty Organization (NATO) assumed responsibility for country-wide security in Afghanistan. But, within several years, terrorist attacks across the country increased. Presidential elections in August 2009 were complicated by many Taliban attacks and bombings. Karzai was once again named the winner and, shortly thereafter, US President Barack Obama stated that he would increase US troops in Afghanistan by thirty thousand.

Triple Agent

On December 30, 2009, tragedy stuck the CIA in Afghanistan. A suicide bomber attacked a facility at Camp Chapman in Khost. Agents at the base provided intelligence to support drone attacks against Taliban members in Pakistan. The attacker, Humam Khalil Abu-Mulal al-Balawi, had been a supporter of al-Qaeda who also worked as a double agent for the CIA. Unbeknownst to the CIA, al-Balawi was still working for al-Qaeda, and was sympathetic to the terrorist cause. Al-Balawi had already provided the CIA with useful information and was invited to the base, as it was believed he had intelligence on senior al-Qaeda leadership.

Because he was trusted, al-Balawi was allowed to enter Camp Chapman without being searched, where he detonated a suicide vest. Seven American CIA agents were killed in the attack, along with a Jordanian

Stars on the CIA Memorial Wall signify agents and contractors who were killed while working for the intelligence agency.

Victory and Defeat

official and an Afghan official. President Obama issued the following statement to CIA employees:

> In recent years, the CIA has been tested as never before. Since our country was attacked on September 11, 2001, you have served on the frontlines in directly confronting the dangers of the twenty-first century. Because of your service, plots have been disrupted, American lives have been saved, and our Allies and partners have been more secure. Your triumphs and even your names may be unknown to your fellow Americans, but your service is deeply appreciated.

The attack sent shockwaves throughout the CIA, dramatically changing the intelligence approach to the war, and culminating in a dramatic increase in the use of drone activity and strikes in the region.

Leakers and Controversies

In 2010, an army intelligence analyst named Chelsea Manning began leaking sensitive and classified documents from online databases. She gave approximately 750,000 documents to the WikiLeaks organization obtained through her access to classified networks such as the Secret Internet Protocol Router Network (SIPRNet), a restricted version of the internet where internal intelligence information an be shared, and the Joint Worldwide Intelligence Communications System (JWICS), a top secret network through which users can transmit especially sensitive information.

The documents and videos showed evidence of war crimes committed by the United States, in particular. For example, one of the most incendiary videos Manning released showed a drone airstrike in Granai, Afghanistan, that killed approximately 140 civilians, 93 of which were children. Manning stated that she had become disillusioned with the war and felt the public needed to learn about US intelligence activities. She served six years in prison and was ultimately found guilty of violating the Espionage Act, which punishes individuals who disclose private information that can jeopardize the United States' relationship with other countries. She was sentenced to thirty-five years in

Chelsea Manning is an American activist.

Victory and Defeat   39

Edward Snowden

Edward Joseph Snowden was born on June 21, 1983, in Elizabeth City, North Carolina. His father was an officer in the US Coast Guard, and his mother worked as a US District Court clerk. During the September 11 attacks, his maternal grandfather was a senior official in the FBI. Snowden joined the Army Reserves in 2004, but was discharged after he broke both his legs in training. Less than ten years later, at twenty-nine years of age, Snowden leaked top-secret government documents, changing the course of history and making his name both revered and loathed.

Snowden was recruited by the CIA for his computer prowess in 2006. He spent six months training at the CIA's secret technology school, and was stationed in Geneva, Switzerland, to maintain security systems there. In 2009, Snowden resigned from the CIA and began working at Dell as a contractor, where he taught top government officials how to prevent hacking on their computers. He rose through the ranks at Dell and began working exclusively with the CIA. Revered as a genius, Snowden was given full administrative privileges to the CIA system, and in 2012, he began downloading classified information.

Disillusionment with US intelligence agencies began for Snowden while working in Geneva. The information he saw through his access at Dell only reinforced his belief that the CIA "was doing far more harm than good." He tried to speak out to his colleagues and bosses, but felt his only choice was to go public. After telling his girlfriend and his employer that he needed to go away to receive medical treatment, he flew to Hong Kong, where he hid out in a hotel room and began leaking documents.

Snowden's actions led to debate about security versus privacy.

The US government, upon learning his identity, charged him with two counts of violating the Espionage Act and one count of theft of government property. In order to escape these charges—and potentially worse charges—he traveled secretly to Russia, where he has been allowed temporary asylum. Snowden asserted he took the risk to leak the documents because he believed the CIA actions "[posed] an existential threat to democracy."

prison, but former president Barack Obama commuted her sentence before he left office in 2017.

Questionable Actions

In 2011, the killing of Anwar al-Awlaki and his son, the first ever Americans targeted by drones, caused outrage within the United States and abroad. Al-Awlaki was targeted for assassination by drones in Yemen, where he escaped after US intelligence agencies accused him of planning attacks for al-Qaeda. Friends and family of al-Awlaki repeatedly stated that he had no connection with the terrorist organization. On September 30, 2011, two Predator drones fired missiles at a car al-Awlaki and three other suspected al-Qaeda members were traveling in. All of them were killed; al-Awlaki and another American man, Samir Khan, among them.

Some people criticized the decision, made at the highest levels of the US government, to assassinate American citizens who were suspected of a crime without a trial. According to lawyer and journalist Glenn Greenwald, this violated the due process clause of the Fifth Amendment, which states that no one should be "deprived of life, liberty, or property, without due process of law." Less than two weeks later, al-Awlaki's sixteen-year-old son Abdulrahman

> **DID YOU KNOW?**
>
> Since 2004 the United States has initiated a total of 406 drone strikes with over 3,000 casualties in Pakistan alone as of 2017.

al-Awlaki was killed in a top-secret CIA drone strike. The CIA later maintained that he had been located near another al-Qaeda member they were targeting, and that he had been killed by accident during that strike.

Victories (?)

Despite the controversies, US intelligence also experienced great success during the war on terror. In the first few months of the American-led invasion of Iraq, Saddam Hussein's government was toppled and the former leader went into hiding. He was the highest-priority figure the CIA was searching for within Iraq. The manhunt to find Hussein was a multi-service mission from the Joint Special Operations Command (JSOC) called Task Force 121. Instead of relying solely on intelligence from drones, however, US secret services conducted raids and hundreds of interrogations with Hussein's known colleagues and friends. One of these men gave up Saddam Hussein's location in a remote hideout just south of his hometown of Tikrit. The location was confirmed through signals intelligence and other spy reconnaissance. Operation Red Dawn was the codename for the mission to target two likely locations for Hussein. Six hundred forces stormed the targets where he was suspected to be hiding on December 13, 2003, and found him hiding in a "spider hole," a small hole hidden under the floorboards of a farmhouse.

Search for Bin Laden

Perhaps the most widely lauded mission during the war on terror was Operation Neptune Spear, a covert mission launched in 2010 to find and capture Osama bin Laden led by the CIA with the JSOC. Efforts leading up to the operation had started nearly ten years earlier, when US intelligence agencies began collecting information on his whereabouts. According to journalist Seymour Hersh, a Pakistani intelligence officer first offered information about bin Laden's location to CIA agents in return for a $25 million reward. This intelligence officer said that bin Laden had been discovered by Pakistani secret service in 2006 and was held under house arrest in Abbottabad.

After the officer passed an advanced polygraph test, the CIA flew drones over the suspected home of bin Laden in order to find evidence of him living there. It was not an easy mission. For one, Bin Laden didn't use cell phones, which the CIA could have used to locate him. He also never left his compound, and never spoke about his location to al-Qaeda members. Instead, he used a trusted courier to send information out to the organization's leaders. Through interrogations of known al-Qaeda members, the United States discovered the names of several potential messengers. When one of the couriers was traced back to bin Laden's suspected compound, operatives were further convinced that they had found the terrorist leader.

For many months, the CIA spent millions of dollars and numerous agency resources in order to further confirm that bin Laden was living there. CIA agents rented a house next door. A NSA program called the Tailored Access Operations group worked to install spyware and tracking devices on targeted computers and phones; using this, they began compiling more information about the residents of the compound. All of this extra data and planning was necessary because the CIA was never able to get a photo of bin Laden at the compound.

Osama bin Laden was captured in a compound in Abbottabad, Pakistan, where he had been hiding for several years.

Perhaps one of the strangest schemes the CIA used to get more evidence about who was living at the compound was a fake hepatitis B vaccination program. CIA agents hired a Pakistani doctor to start a vaccination drive in the city, which would seem authentic enough that bin Laden's family would open their doors to the doctor. They hoped that, if the doctor indeed gave vaccinations to the people living in the compound, they would be able to collect their DNA to test and determine whether or not bin Laden lived there. It is still not clear if this program succeeded or failed, but regrettably the plan was uncovered and publicized, leading to a lasting impact on global health. Most notably, in years following the incident, health workers in Pakistan attempting to administer polio vaccines were banned and even killed, forcing the United Nations to withdraw aid. The effects of the decline in vaccinations due to distrust in the area are still being examined in 2017.

Kill or Capture

High-level meetings in the White House were organized to discuss what to do with incoming information regarding bin Laden. In April 2011, following a series of meetings with the National Security Council, President Barack Obama decided to move forward with a helicopter raid, and a special operative Sea Air and Land (SEAL) team was selected—although they weren't told the specifics of the mission, or whom they were capturing. In order to maintain security, the operation was also planned without the knowledge of the Pakistani military and needed to be done quickly and quietly. On the night of May 1, the attack began.

Two dozen US Navy SEALs landed newly developed stealth helicopters, which were quieter and harder to see on radar, within and near the compound. SEALs wore night-vision goggles and carried assault rifles, machine guns, and grenades, along with other gear. Drone video was transmitted back to the

Situation Room at the White House, where President Barack Obama and other top officials were watching for updates. Fighter jets and drones flew above the compound for support. By the end of the short raid, bin Laden had been shot and killed. When President Obama announced the execution of the raid and the death of the al-Qaeda leader later that night, cheers erupted around the United States and abroad.

An Ethical Dilemma

Despite the victories gained through drone use, many publically questioned the CIA assassination program carried out by weaponized flyers. Drone attacks continued to gain negative press, like that in Datta Khel, Pakistan, on March 17, 2011. The attack was intended for a compound suspected to contain Taliban members, but an estimated forty-two people were killed and others injured. Although governments disagree on the exact number of innocent casualties, women and the elderly with no links to known or suspected terrorist organizations were among those that died. Thousands of protestors took to the streets following the attack, and eventually the Pakistan military issued a statement in December 2011 that US drones would be shot down.

In 2012, researchers from New York University and Stanford University determined that US drone attacks had killed many more civilians than had been officially disclosed. The researchers discovered that these drones "were nowhere near as discriminating toward noncombatants" as claimed by CIA officials. Another study by the New American Foundation "concluded that drones probably killed some two hundred and fifty to three hundred civilians in the decade leading up to 2014."

Lethal Precision

Starting in 2014, civilian casualties in CIA-directed drone attacks decreased significantly. This was due in large part to the development of a new generation of armed drone, called the General Atomics MQ-9 Reaper. The Reaper can fly at speeds of around 230 miles per hour (370 kmh) and has a range of approximately 1,150 miles (1,851 km). According to CIA officials, the Reaper is a more reliable and high-tech drone, which uses different sensors to provide high-resolution data to operators. For example, the MTS-C sensor allows drone operators to track unfired missiles and warheads, as well as exhaust and fumes from these weapons. Many Reapers also have automatic takeoff and landing capacities.

Reapers also carry a range of weapons, including laser-guided bombs and air-to-ground missiles, in addition to high-resolution cameras and sensors. According to one CIA agent, "The Reaper can also fire a missile, known as the Small Smart Weapon, that is less than two feet long (sixty-one centimeters) and can take out an individual without killing people in the next room." While drones have become more exact and have decreased the number of civilians accidently killed during strikes, the legality of such targeted assassinations is still in question. Of course, drones are also still used for surveillance-only purposes. In 2013, FBI director Robert Mueller admitted that the United States uses drones not only abroad during the war on terror, but also within the United States to aid in surveillance.

The Islamic State

In 2014, peacekeepers with NATO left Afghanistan, but the war was not over. In fact, 2014 proved to be the deadliest year in Afghanistan since 2001, with multiple terrorist attacks being carried out every day. A new terrorist organization emerging in Syria during the civil war, known as the Islamic State (IS), also surfaced in Afghanistan and Iraq. The Islamic State carried out

> **DID YOU KNOW?**
>
> Although originally formed as a branch of al-Qaeda in Iraq, the Islamic State formally separated from the terrorist organization in 2014 after disagreements among militants in the groups.

many attacks across Iraq and Syria and successfully captured important territories across the region. In 2015, US President Barack Obama declared that he would delay troop withdrawal from Afghanistan. US involvement in the war in Afghanistan has continued to the present day.

US air strikes in Iraq in 2016 pushed IS back from strongholds, and the new Taliban leader, Mullah Mansour, was killed in May in a US drone attack. However, IS attacks continued, both within war-torn areas of the Middle East and without. In June 2017, IS fighters captured the Tora Bora region of Afghanistan, which houses a military base that was previously used by al-Qaeda leader Osama bin Laden. Individual attacks by IS militants, and those inspired by the terrorist organization, also continue across the world.

Victory and Defeat

Stuxnet is a malicious computer program, also known as a worm, designed to spread through machines that met specific requirements once introduced through an infected flash drive. Windows operating systems and programmable logic controllers (PLCs) were among the vulnerable digital systems. PLCs can automate electrical or mechanical tasks, and were used in Iranian nuclear labs. Infected PLCs caused nuclear centrifuges to spin much faster than normal, and approximately one-fifth of all Iranian nuclear centrifuges were broken by Stuxnet in this way.

Stuxnet was eventually discovered in 2010 due to an error in its code that allowed it to travel outside of the Iranian nuclear system and into computers around the world. Following information available in leaked documents, investigative reports, and statements made by various government officials, it was revealed that Stuxnet was developed by the NSA, CIA, and Israeli intelligence; however, neither the Unites States nor Israel has made an official admission.

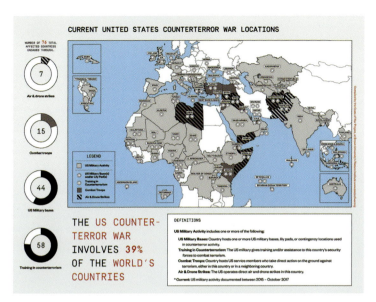

This illustration from the Watson Institute shows the scope of US war on terror as of 2017.

While high-tech surveillance has continued to be controversial, most analysts agree that it has thwarted many potential terrorist attacks since September 11, 2001. Countries like the United States are still struggling to find a balance between effective intelligence through technological innovations and the human right to privacy. No country has—as of yet—found a satisfactory answer to this question, which may be the largest ethical dilemma of our time.

Victory and Defeat

CHAPTER 4

IMPACT AND LEGACY

While the global war on terror is far from over, official US combat operations have lessened in both Afghanistan and Iraq. US troops lend support to Afghani and Iraqi forces as needed, including for training and strategic purposes, and the United States continues to provide weapons and surveillance in these regions. Instead of participating in organized warfare, America's role in the continued war on terror is more nebulous and intelligence based. In fact, much criticism has been launched against US agencies for focusing on technology-driven surveillance instead of diplomacy and conventional reconnaissance.

OPPOSITE:
Former President George W. Bush signs the Patriot Act into law on October 26, 2001.

Alex Finley, formerly an officer of CIA's Directorate of Operations, published an article in *POLITICO* magazine titled "How the CIA Forgot the Art of Spying," in which she maintains that surveillance technology, at which the United States has excelled, has led to a lack of traditional spying techniques that, in fact, might be more useful in the global war on terror.

> The new [terror] threat demanded a new way of spying. What the classic Cold War spycraft officers had painstakingly learned didn't help in this new mission. Attending soirees and rubbing elbows with international VIPs wasn't how you tracked down terrorists, who hid in hillsides and remote compounds in hostile territory. Chalk marks on a street lamp to signal a meeting; dead drops in a park, filled or emptied after hours traipsing through a bustling city to determine whether you were under surveillance—these techniques now seemed obsolete. The new kind of spying ... was done by officers based in military compounds, only able to leave with a Glock on the hip, in armored personnel carriers, guarded by armed men and women in uniforms with the American flag sewn on the arm.

During the Cold War, CIA and NSA agents honed their skills and learned how to assess and develop human sources of information. Spies underwent psychological and language training to fit into the culture. During the global war on terror, and with the ease of these new technologies, US intelligence agencies have focused less on personalized spying techniques in favor of long-distance or impersonal surveillance. However, as IS has become dispersed and disjointed, and so-called lone wolf attacks have become more common, the importance of forming relationships within communities and understanding cultural traditions and expectations has increased. Drones can perhaps locate a bomb-making facility in war-torn Iraq, but are not very useful when it comes to discovering specific individuals with no known connection to terrorist groups who are working alone.

The New Surveillance Market

The changes in CIA tactics following attacks on September 11 led to an increase in the private security industry and private military companies operating in and on behalf of the United States, as well as around the world. The war on terror, and the Iraq War in particular, created a much larger market for private military contractors (PMCs) and their services. While that may sound like a good thing, it also led to problems within US intelligence communities. Agents and spies could make more money in the private sector than in the public sector and left in droves, particularly older and more experienced agents. According to Finley, "By 2005, half of the CIA's workforce—operators and analysts alike—had five years' experience or less." This hindered operations and further shifted the way intelligence agencies collected information.

One solution to the problems that have plagued the CIA and other intelligence agencies is to return to more traditional spying techniques—while keeping the competitive edge on new technology. As Finley states, "The pivot back toward traditional espionage will be a shock to the system, but a necessary one."

Permitted Intrusion

A return to more conventional methods may also help regain the trust of US intelligence agencies in the eyes of the American public. After the US government began secret surveillance and data collection programs following the terrorist attacks on September 11, 2001, Americans did not know the extent to which their personal data was being collected and shared. This changed, of course, after several whistleblowers released top-secret information about these anti-terrorism programs to the American public. Despite the fact that these surveillance programs were not technically permitted by the US Constitution and Bill of Rights, several national security acts, including the USA Patriot Act, the PRECISE Act, and the FISA Amendment Act, allowed these programs to continue, and the practice of government agencies and private corporations to monitor, mine, and use electronic information is a topic continually under debate.

Additional Surveillance Disclosures

On June 13, 2013, documents detailing the extent of surveillance programs were first published in *The Guardian*, making a historical impact on discussions around mass surveillance. The information had been released to the newspaper by Edward Snowden. *Guardian* journalist Glenn Greenwald was initially contacted by Snowden anonymously in 2012, using encrypted email. Snowden knew that as soon as he released these documents he could be prosecuted for stealing sensitive data from the US government, and even for treason. In addition, he would be at risk of being targeted for execution by intelligence agents

TrackMeNot

Governments are not the only ones amassing hoards of online data from users around the globe—so are corporations. Search engines like Google and social networking apps gather data from devices and then target advertisements based on search history, age, gender, and other information collected. Generally companies like Google do not sell personal information to corporate advertisers, but they do show links to products that they think a user would be interested in based on surfing history. Once a link is clicked and results in a purchase as an outcome of this profiling, the benefitting company will pay a small fee to Google. Google makes millions—if not billions—of dollars in revenue from this.

But some people don't like thinking that online movements are being tracked, and feel that their privacy is being invaded. Targeted ads can also become annoying and emotionally triggering. Many people also fear that their tracked online history will eventually be sold or collected by the US government. That's why New York University professor Helen Nissenbaum and researcher and technologist Daniel C. Howe came up with TrackMeNot.

Nissenbaum came up with the idea for the anti-tracking application after learning about a technique used by World War II fighter pilots. In order to confuse the enemy's radar systems, pilots would release foil

Helen Nissenbaum co-created TrackMeNot in order to prevent commercial internet data collection.

paper creating so many false signals that the enemy wouldn't know where to direct its anti-aircraft missiles. In a similar way, the TrackMeNot website states the program "hides users' actual search trails in a cloud of 'ghost' queries, significantly increasing the difficulty of aggregating such data into accurate or identifying user profiles." While it does not actively prevent information gathering, "TrackMeNot serves as a means of amplifying users' discontent with advertising networks that not only disregard privacy, but also facilitate the bulk surveillance agendas of corporate and government agencies, as documented recently in disclosures by Edward Snowden and others."

once his identity was disclosed. Later he stated, "All I can say right now is the US government is not going to be able to cover this up by jailing or murdering me. Truth is coming, and it cannot be stopped."

Snowden and Greenwald, aided also by journalist Laura Poitras and others, began to comb though the hundreds of thousands of documents to decide what to release. They wanted to redact any information on secret service agents who could be at risk if their identities were known. Furthermore, they did not want to put countries like the United States in danger. So they released documents could not include personal information, very sensitive defense details, or other evidence that could jeopardize the safety of others. Following the first publication, other media outlets also released the selected documents and reported on stories regarding US and global surveillance programs.

DID YOU KNOW?

During the making of the 2016 film *Snowden* staring Joseph Gordon-Levitt, Snowden himself was an advisor, and helped with details such as realistic CIA computer screens and hacker lingo.

Electronic Eyes Everywhere

Over the series of exposés, many classified programs of which the public had no previous knowledge were revealed. Among them was the global surveillance program carried out by NSA with the aid and cooperation of Australia, the UK, and Canada's secret service. Another was a program under the code name PRISM, which allowed the US government direct access to American's Google and Yahoo email accounts following a top-secret court decision. Also under PRISM, American courts had required service providers like Verizon and AT&T to hand over phone call logs of regular Americans to the NSA every day. A new tool called Boundless Informant had likewise been developed and used by the NSA.

According to documents released by Snowden, Boundless Informant counted and analyzed internet and telephone metadata records secretly. All of this was analyzed and stored in an NSA data archive. Similarly, XKeyscore (XKS) enabled NSA analysts to search and analyze global internet data on a daily basis. XKS operates as a search engine, much like Google, for NSA analysts. Working with other systems, it can produce online attacks against targets, such as when one target is communicating with a known terrorist. This data is then immediately brought to the attention of officials. XKS is housed at around 150 sites in countries all over the world, particularly in US embassies and consulates. It works with and analyzes data from satellites, telecommunications providers, and internet metadata, in addition to spy planes and drones.

Technology developed to collect internet and phone data includes Carnivore, ECHELON, and NarusInsight. These systems and others also have various functions including: speech-to-text programs; social network analysis to determine patterns on social media between online friends; and "human identification at a distance," which uses people's own cameras on computers and phones to take pictures of and identify who is using the equipment. Programs like "Magic Lantern" and CIPAV, which the FBI and other agencies can install remotely on a computer system, can monitor an individual's personal computer use, including financial records, Google searches, and photos.

All of this is just for the collection of phone and internet data by US intelligence agencies. Other high-tech programs and algorithms gather information both in the United States and around the world. For instance, the US Postal Service takes a photo of every single piece of mail sent within the United States every day and logs it into a searchable system.

Under Constant Watch

Even when a person is not using a computer, mobile device, or smartphone, Americans are being surveyed. Wide Area Motion Imaging (WAMI) is the name for a program that uses airborne and satellite imaging to see patterns on the streets of major cities and metro areas. For example, any and every pedestrian and car in New York City, within the field of view of this system, would be tracked. The advanced algorithms the system uses allows automated and searchable geo-location. WAMI sensors are mounted on airplanes, drones, blimps, and helicopters and can cover about 70 sq mi (181 sq km) at a time. In some cases, mayors and other

Cameras installed across cities and towns can provide real-time video to law enforcement and government agencies.

elected officials of these localities are unaware of the spying programs over their own cities. In addition, surveillance cameras and traffic cameras are mounted in most urban areas. These cover the streets at ground level, and videos and photos captured by these systems can be sent to law enforcement and government agencies when necessary.

Debatable Legality

The problem with many of these programs, as reported by the media, was that it was an indiscriminate mass collection. This means that US intelligence agencies and foreign agencies did not get warrants or provide evidence to target suspected terrorists. Rather, it was a blanket spying program that collected data from everyone, with no verification that this type of data collection was necessary.

Almost immediately after these classified operations were made public, critics spoke out, questioning the constitutionality of the programs. In particular, stating that the mass surveillance went against the Fourth Amendment of the US Constitution, which protects: "The right of the people to be secure in their persons, houses, papers, and effects, against unreasonable searches and seizures, shall not be violated, and no Warrants shall issue, but upon probably cause, supported by Oath or affirmation, and particularly describing the place to be searched, and the persons or things to be seized."

On November 9, 2015, Richard Leon, a federal US district court judge in the District of Columbia, issued a ruling condemning the actions of the Obama administration and the NSA.

> The Fourth Amendment typically requires a "neutral and detached authority be interposed between the police and the public," and it is offended by "general warrants" and laws that allow searches to be conducted 'indiscriminately and without regard to their connections with a crime under investigation." ... I cannot imagine a more "indiscriminate" and "arbitrary invasion" than this systematic and high-tech collection and retention of personal data on virtually every single citizen for purposes of querying and analyzing it without prior judicial approval. Surely such a program infringes on "that degree of privacy" that the founders enshrined in the Fourth Amendment.

Leon also asserted that his ruling "will not, however, be the last chapter in the ongoing struggle to balance privacy rights and national security

The NSA use of cell phone data has been very controversial, with many public figures speaking out against it.

interests under our Constitution in an age of evolving technological wizardry."

Due in part to the outrage created by Snowden's leak, when certain parts of the Patriot Act expired in 2015, they were not renewed. This included the end of bulk collection of phone metadata by the NSA. However, bulk collection of data by phone companies was allowed to continue, with intelligence agencies able access to this data on a case-by-case basis.

The Future of Warfare

Intelligence communities have maintained that the next generation of spying and warfare will take place almost entirely in cyberspace. Indeed, cyber attacks have been growing, and the United States and other countries have ramped up both defensive and offensive capabilities online. The United States Cyber Command (USCYBERCOM) was created in 2009 and is an independent command under the US Department of Defense. USCYBERCOM "plans, coordinates, integrates, synchronizes and conducts activities to: direct the operations and defense of specified Department of Defense information networks and; prepare to, and when directed, conduct full spectrum military cyberspace operations in order to enable actions in all domains, ensure US/Allied freedom of action in cyberspace and deny the same to our adversaries."

Since more spying techniques and operations are being moved to the cyber world, this is the logical place where the battles of the future will be fought. The modern world of warfare is very different from wars in the past. Traditional battlefields and spying activities—whether for better or worse—have been relegated to the sidelines. Today, remote controlled machines can be killers, and information gathering and espionage occurs through high-tech programs and computer viruses that can cause damage or even harm or kill. Will we be better off for these new developments in spying and warfare? The question remains a complicated one, but one that warrants continued attempts to solve, even if no neat solutions are to be found.

Thwarting Lone Wolf Attacks

In the wake of devastating attacks, such as the attack outside the Houses of Parliament in London in March 2017 that left five dead, intelligence communities and the police are speaking out about the difficulty of stopping "low-level" incidents, committed by one individual. While groups like al-Qaeda and IS can be surveilled, infiltrated, and tracked, small scale terrorist activities are especially difficult to prevent. According to Daniel L. Byman, a senior fellow in foreign policy at the Brookings Institute, "the year 2016 was the year of the Lone Wolf terrorist" when these kinds of attacks dramatically increased across the world.

While Byman maintains lone wolf attackers cannot be completely stopped, incidents can be reduced. He states, "the less [lone wolves] can interact with potential co-conspirators, and in particular with dangerous groups that give them direction and training, the less dangerous they will be. Intelligence gathering and arrests of suspected cell leaders and targeting terrorist command and control via drone strikes is thus vital . . . US intelligence should [also] continue to exploit social media to identify potential group members and to disrupt their activities." Lone wolf attacks are also a sign of larger organizational weakness, like the Islamic State as it is being routed out of territory in the Middle East. This presents an opportunity to plant disinformation into the

On March 22, 2017, a lone wolf attacker killed two in an attack outside London's Houses of Parliament.

Islamic State's network, and further disrupt its larger operations.

Perhaps the greatest obstacle to thwarting lone wolf attacks are increasing levels of Islamophobia, or a fear of Muslim people and their religion. Byman asserts, "This Islamophobia, in turn, can begin a dangerous circle. As communities become suspect, they withdraw into themselves and become less trustful of law enforcement. They provide fewer tips and otherwise are reluctant to point out the bad apples among them . . . Such problems risk fundamental changes in politics and undermine liberal democracy." One counter measure as Byman sees it, is "to ensure community support from Muslims living in the United States . . . [since] good community relations minimize motivations for violence and encourage local cooperation with authorities."

Chronology

1990 Saddam Hussein invades Kuwait

1991 The United States and allied forces deploy to Saudi Arabi. The Gulf War comes to an end after just over five weeks.

1993 Al-Qaeda-trained terrorists plant a bomb in the World Trade Center.

2001 On September 11, al-Qaeda terrorists crash planes into the World Trade Center and the Pentagon. The US War in Afghanistan begins. On October 26, the USA Patriot Act is passed by Congress.

2003 The Iraq War begins on March 19. Saddam Hussein is captured on December 13.

2006 Saddam Hussein is executed. Al-Qaeda leader Abu Musab al-Zarqawi is killed in Iraq during a US attack.

2010 US Army service member Chelsea Manning releases classified documents from internal servers to WikiLeaks.

2011 US troops officially withdraw from Iraq. Operation Neptune Spear ends with the death of Osama bin Laden.

2013 Chelsea Manning is convicted of violations against the Espionage Act. Edward Snowden releases classified information about US surveillance programs.

2014 As US troops withdrawl from Afghanistan, terrorist activity in the country increases. The Islamic State gains attention as it captures important territories in Iraq.

2017 President Barack Obama commutes Chelsea Manning's sentence.

Glossary

analog Relating to or using signals from variable physical quantities, such as voltage or location.

assets A useful thing or person; in intelligence communities, people who offer information about suspicious activities.

digital Relating to storing information in the form of digital signals, or signals expressed as 0s and 1s.

electromechanical Relating to an electronically operated mechanical device.

espionage The practice, typically by governments or companies, to obtain information through spies or the use of spy technology.

high-resolution A high degree of detail available in photos or video.

intelligence analyst A person who analyzes and interprets data for intelligence purposes.

nebulous Vague or undefined.

network A group of interconnected people or things, such as computers, broadcasting stations, or spies.

polygraph test A machine that can record changes in a person's pulse or breathing rates to determine if they are telling a lie.

protocols A set of rules for exchanging information between computing devices.

proximity Nearness.

satellite A manmade object launched into space in order to collect data or for communication.

signals intelligence Information gathering by intercepting and monitoring communications, often involving cryptanalysts to decipher messages.

thermal Relating to heat.

ultimatum A final demand.

unwieldy Too large.

warheads The explosive part of a missile or torpedo.

weaponized Converted to be used as a weapon.

Further Information

Books

Curley, Rob. *Spy Agencies, Intelligence Operations, and the People Behind Them*. Chicago, IL: Britannica Educational Publishing, 2014.

Nardo, Don. *Cause and Effect: The War on Terror*. San Diego, CA: ReferencePoint Press, 2018.

Yomtov, Nelson. *War on Terror Technology*. Minneapolis, MN: Core Library, 2018.

Websites

Electronic Freedom Foundation
https://www.eff.org
The EFF is a leading non-profit organization dedicated to protecting digital privacy and free speech in the age of mass surveillance.

The Intercept
https://theintercept.com
Founded by journalists Glenn Greenwald, Laura Poitras, and Jeremy Scahill, this site offers a forum for investigative journalists to report with editorial freedom.

National Security Agency
https://www.nsa.gov
Learn more about the NSA, their unclassified missions, and their leadership at their official website.

Selected Bibliography

ABC News. "Smarter Weapons for a New Gulf War." Retrieved November 11, 2017. https://www.abcnews.go.com/technology/story?id=97718&page=1.

Andrews, Evan. "Who Invented the Internet?" History: Ask History, December 18, 2013. http://www.history.com/news/ask-history/who-invented-the-internet.

BBC. "Drones: What Are They and How Do They Work?" BBC: South Asia, January 31, 2012. https://www.bbc.com/news/world-south-asia-10713898.

Byman, Daniel L. "Can Lone Wolves Be Stopped?" Brookings Institute, March 15, 2017. https://www.brookings.edu/blog/markaz/2017/03/15/can-lone-wolves-be-stopped.

Citino, Robert. "Technology in the Persian Gulf War of 1991." The Gilder Lehrman Institute of American History. Retrieved November 11, 2017. https://www.gilderlehrman.org/history-by-era/facing-new-millennium/essays/technology-persian-gulf-war-1991.

Coll, Steve. "The Unblinking Stare." New Yorker, November 24, 2014. https://www.newyorker.com/magazine/2014/11/24/unblinking-stare.

Curiosity. "TrackMeNot Helps Cover Your Online Trail." Curiosity. Retrieved November 24, 2017. https://curiosity.com/topics/trackmenot-helps-cover-your-online-trail-curiosity.

Finley, Alex. "How the CIA Forgot the Art of Spying." POLITICO, March/April 2017. https://www.politico.com/magazine/story/2017/cia-art-spying-espionage-spies-military-terrorism-214875.

Greenwald, Glenn, Swen MacAskill and Laura Poitras. "Edward Snowden: The Whistleblower Behind the NSA Surveillance Revelations." The Guardian, June 11, 2013. https://www.theguardian.com/world/2013/jan/09/Edward-snowden-nsa-whistleblower-surveillance.

Goldman, Joshua. "Best Toy Drones You Can Buy Right Now." CNET, April 14, 2016. https://www.cnet.com/news/best-toy-drones.

Moseman, Andrew. "Body of Lies' Spy Tech is Closer to Reality Than Bond. Popular Mechanics, September 30, 2009. https://www.popularmechanics.com/military/a12130/4286845.

Patterson, Thom. "1970s Spy Satellite 'Better Than Google Earth'." CNN, September 1, 2016. https://www.cnn.com/2016/09/01/declassified-spy-satellite-hexagon/index.html.

Shachtman, Noah. "How Technology Almost Los the War: In Iraq, the Critical Networks are Social—Not Electronic." Wired, November 27, 2007. https://www.wiredcom/2007/11/ff-futurewar.

Talbot, David. "How Technology Failed in Iraq." Technology Review, November 1, 2004. https://www.technologyreview.com/403319/how-technology-failed-in-iraq.

Index

Page numbers in **boldface** are illustrations.

Advanced Research Projects Agency Network (ARPANET), 9
al-Qaeda, 18, 21, 23, 37, 42–43, 45, 48, 51 ,70
analog, 6
assassination, 42, 48, 50
assets, 29

bin Laden, Osama, 18, **19**, 21, 34, 36, 44–48, 51

Central Intelligence Agency (CIA), 9, 20, 28–29, 33–38, 40–41, 43–46, 48–50, 52, 56–58, 62
Cold War, 9, 25, 56–57
Colossus, 7–8, **7**
computers, 5–9, 21, 24, 28, 40, 45, 52, 62, 64–65, 69
cyber attacks, 68–69

digital, 8, 13, 52
diplomacy, 55
drones (see Unmanned Aerial Vehicle (UAV))
drones, toy, 26–27, **27**
due process, 42

electromechanical, 6–7
espionage, 9, 11–12, 24, 58, 69
Espionage Act, 39, 41

evidence, 39, 45–46, 62, 66

Federal Bureau of Investigation (FBI), 20, 40, 50, 64
Fourth Amendment, 66–67

hackers, 24, 28, 40, 62
high-resolution, 5, 26, 49–50

intelligence analyst, 38
internet, 5, 8–9, 21, 28, 39, 63–64
Islamic State (IS), 23, 50–51, 57, 70–71
Islamophobia, 71

Joint Special Operations Command (JSOC), 43–44

leak, 28, 38, 40–41, 52, 68
lone wolf attacks, 57, 70–71

Manning, Chelsea, 38–39, **39**

National Security Agency (NSA), 20, 45, 52, 57, 63, 67–68
nebulous, 55
network, 9, 21, 28, 39, 60–61, 64, 69, 71

Operation Desert Storm, 11, 14

Operation Enduring Freedom, 22, 35
Operation Freedom's Sentinel, 23
Operation Iraqi Freedom, 23
Operation Neptune Spear, 44

personal information, 58, 60, 62, 64, 67
playing cards, 32, **32**
polygraph test, 45
precision guided munitions (PGMs), 13
PRISM, 63
privacy, right to, 53, 60–61, 67
private military contractors (PMCs), 57–58
programmable logic controllers (PLCs), 52
protocols, 9, 39
proximity, 10

satellite, **4**, 5, 13–15, 64–65
Short-Range Agent Communications, 9–10
signals intelligence, 44
Snowden, Edward, 28, 40–41, **41**, 59, 61–63, 68
Sombolay, Albert, 12
Stuxnet, 52
surveillance, 24, 28, 31, 53, 55–59, 61–63, 66, 70

Taliban, 21–22, 33–36, 48, 51
technology, 5–6, 8, 10, 13–15, 24–25, 36, 53, 55–58, 64, 68
text messaging, 8–9
thermal, 14
TrackMeNot, 60–61

ultimatum, 21
Unmanned Aerial Vehicle (UAV), 15, 25–26, 28, 33–36, 38, 42–43, 45, 47–50, 57, 64–65, 70: drone strikes, 34–35, 38–39, 43, 48–51, 70; Predator, 33–35, **34**, 42; Reaper, 49–50
unwieldy, 24
US Central Command (CENTCOM), 35
USA Patriot Act, 20–21, 59, 68

video, 25–26, 34, 39, 47, 66
virus (computer), 69

war crimes, 39
warheads, 49
weaponized, 48
weapons of mass destruction (WMDs), 23
Wide Area Motion Imaging (WAMI), 65
WikiLeaks, 28–29, 38

XKeyscore (XKS), 63–64

Index 79

About the Author

Elizabeth Schmermund is a writer, editor, and researcher who has authored more than twenty titles for young adults. Her academic research focuses in the role of women in the 2003 Iraq War. She is both fascinated and horrified by new technologies that have been developed for modern warfare.